The Berenstain Bears® at BIG BEAR FAIR

Stan & Jan Berenstain

A GOLDEN BOOK • NEW YORK

Western Publishing Company, Inc., Racine, Wisconsin 53404

Tan-ta-ra!

Rum-tum-tum!

Blow the horn.

Beat the drum.

Happy music
fills the air!
It brings a smile
to every bear!

So welcome, friends,
to fun, fun, fun!
The Big Bear Fair
has just begun!

BABY PIG?
PIGLET!
BABY COW?
CALF!
BABY SHEEP?
LAMB!
BABY DUCK?
DUCKLING!
Professor Wise
knows all the answers!
Professor Wise

Sister has her
fortune told.

Brother Bear
tests his aim
at the baseball
throwing game.

Look! Brother has won
a super prize—
a big green troll
with purple eyes!

Ralph Ripoff,
of shell game fame,
is living up
to his name.

There's lots of food
at the fair
to suit the taste
of every bear.

Cotton candy,

burgers,

fries,

footlong hot dogs,

homemade pies.

And lots and lots
and *lots* of flies!

There are many rides
at the fair
to suit the taste
of every bear.

Some are slow.

Some are quick.

Some can make you very sick!

But at the fair
the main event
takes place inside
the big fair tent.

These two judges
are just about
to give the prize
blue ribbons out.

First they look at
the fancy chair
that Papa made
just for the fair.

Then they see some
other chairs
nicely made
by other bears.

But Papa wins
that ribbon blue!
And Mama wins
a ribbon, too—

for one of her
very special dishes!
The judges thought
it quite delicious!

Farmer Ben wins
a ribbon for
Sir William Prince,
his giant boar.

Look over there!
The big fair judge
is about to taste
Mrs. Ben's chocolate fudge.

The judge says, "Mmmm!"

She rolls her eyes.

Hooray! Mrs. Ben

also wins a prize!

What a day
this has been!
All we've done
is win, win, win!

We head for home.
The day is done.
We're glad you came
and hope that you had
fun, fun, fun!